3-3-11

The Goodbye Cancer Garden

Janna Matthies   Illustrated by Kristi Valiant

Albert Whitman & Company, Chicago, Illinois

Library of Congress Cataloging-in-Publication Data

Matthies, Janna.
The "Goodbye Cancer" garden / by Janna Matthies ; illustrated by Kristi Valiant.
p. cm.
Summary: When a mother is diagnosed with breast cancer, she and her family plant
a garden and watch it grow through the seasons as she undergoes treatments
and gets better.
ISBN 978-0-8075-2994-2
[1. Cancer—Fiction. 2. Gardening—Fiction. 3. Gardens—Fiction. 4. Family life—Fiction.]
I. Valiant, Kristi, ill. II. Title.
PZ7.M4352Go 2011 [E]—dc22 2010024069

The design is by Carol Gildar.

For more information about Albert Whitman & Company,
please visit our web site at www.albertwhitman.com.

For everyone who walked through the valley with us,
and for those who journey there now (Psalm 23).—J.M.

In memory of Aunt Janell.—K.V.

In our backyard, where first base used to be, is a special garden. We didn't expect to plant it. But Mom says things don't always go as expected.

For example, Mom didn't expect the doctor to say she had breast cancer. But in January, with the backyard under a blanket of snow, she and Dad told us the news.

For a few weeks Mom went back and forth to the hospital for x-rays and tests. Sometimes she looked sad, and my brother and I felt a little worried. So one day we all went together to meet Mom's doctor.

"You must be Janie and Jeffrey," the doctor said. "I've heard lots about you."

"Is Mom better yet?" Jeffrey asked.

"Not yet," she said. "But we're working very hard to make her better—probably by pumpkin time."

Jeffrey smiled. "Pumpkins? I love pumpkins!"

That gave me an idea . . .

On Valentine's Day we helped Mom pack an overnight bag for the hospital. The next day she was having an operation to take the cancer out.

"Things are going to be tough for a while," Dad said. "But Janie's thought of a way to help."

I led everyone to the window and pointed at the hard February ground. "Let's plant a garden!" I said. "Watching it grow, and eating healthy veggies, will remind us Mom's getting better. Then before we know it . . . *Hello, pumpkins, goodbye cancer!*"

Mom reached her arms around us. "The Goodbye Cancer Garden," she said. "What a perfect idea."

After the operation it took a month of arm stretches
before Mom could hug us again. The doctor said no lifting, so
friends and family started dropping by with groceries and
big pots of *yummy-smelling* food.

Our neighbors brought a surprise for me to put on
Mom's head.
"We're here to serve the queen!" they said.
Mom's eyes sparkled. And soon, so did our house.

One sunny Saturday in March, Dad and Jeffrey dug
the vegetable bed while Mom and I drew a map.
"Everybody choose two vegetables," I said.
I already knew mine—cucumbers and tomatoes.

"I want carrots and cherries," Jeffrey said. Dad explained that cherries are a fruit and grow on trees. Jeffrey chose green beans instead. Dad decided on lettuce and potatoes.

"Hmmm," Mom said. "I'll do peppers and . . . oh . . . we almost forgot! Peppers and especially *pumpkins!*"

In April Mom started chemotherapy, a super-strong medicine that destroys leftover bits of cancer. When she felt too sick to eat dinner, Dad made her applesauce. When she was too tired to get out of bed, I showed her seed catalogs and Jeffrey drew her pictures.

When the doctor said soon the chemo would make her hair fall out, Mom said, "Let's have a head-shaving party!"

We tied ribbons around Mom's curls, for us to cut and keep. Then *my* uncle shaved her hair closer than his buzz cut.

"You look weird, Mom," Jeffrey said.

Dad and I thought she looked beautiful.

By May, the last frost had come and gone and Mom was tired of being cooped up inside.

"We're going to the garden store!" she announced.

The store was alive with colors and smells. While Mom rested on a bench, Dad and I piled the cart with plants, soil, and mulch.

"Where's Jeffrey?" Mom said.

"Under here!" he called.

Mom laughed. "I like your green wig. Can I borrow it sometime?"

The next weekend we put in the baby plants first—tomatoes and peppers. Then we traced lines in the dirt for the carrot and lettuce seeds. Next we built a bamboo tower and pushed in cucumber seeds around it. Finally we poked holes and dropped in beans and bits of sprouting potato.

"Last but not least," Mom said, "I will personally plant the pumpkin seeds!"

Just in time for summer, the doctor changed Mom's chemo medicine. Sometimes her bones ached or her feet tingled, but that didn't stop her from doing a little weeding and watering.

In June we played baseball every night after dinner and hit a few foul balls into the garden.

"Look—flowers!" Jeffrey said. "And tiny tomatoes!" I patted the leafy plants and whispered, "Keep up the good work."

In July we drove thirteen hours to my grandparents' house near the beach.

"Salt water and sunshine are just what you need," Grandpa told Mom.

I took pictures of Mom under the umbrella with my baby cousin, rubbing sunscreen on their matching heads. And each day we collected shiny treasures to take home for decorating the garden.

Pulling back into the driveway, we were amazed.
The garden had grown into a jungle!

Best of all was August. We celebrated the end of chemo with a picnic and invited everyone who had helped us.

We served cream cheese and cucumber sandwiches; potato salad; pickled green beans; tossed salad with lettuce, peppers, and tomatoes; and carrot juice.

"Did you grow all this yourself?" my friend Nikki asked.

"Not everything," Jeffrey said. "We don't know how to grow cream cheese yet."

In September Mom started radiation treatments five days a week. The doctor said shining x-ray beams where the cancer had been would help keep it from coming back. Mom said it felt like having a sunburn.

Jeffrey and I also started something—a new year of school. One morning Mom and I helped Jeffrey carry in a tray of homegrown carrots to share at snack time.

"I want to be a carrot farmer when I grow up," Jeffrey said to his teacher.

"Looks like you already are," she said.

There under the classroom lights, we could all see a new crop of fuzz growing on Mom's head.

By the middle of October, Mom was finally done with cancer treatment. "How about we celebrate with a little baseball?" she said. Right away Jeffrey whacked a foul ball into the garden.

"What's that over there?" I said, tiptoeing through the vines toward something big and orange.

There, under elephant-ear leaves,
lay two perfect pumpkins.

"Pumpkins!" Jeffrey and I yelled at the same time.

Mom blinked away happy tears. "How could we have forgotten?" she said. The four of us pulled at the pumpkins with all our might and landed in a big heap, right in the middle of the Goodbye Cancer Garden.

We spent the rest of the day making
pumpkin bread and roasting pumpkin seeds.
But not all the seeds. Some we let dry in the sun,
for growing more pumpkins next year.